DRAGON SLAYER
OF THE PINK SAND DEAD SEA DESERT

G.G. GARTH

Jumpmaster Press
Birmingham, AL

Copyright

Dragon Slayer of the Pink Sale Dead Sea Desert – A *Coronial* Fairy Tale, by G.G. Garth

Copyright ©2021 G.G. Garth a/k/a Ghia Szwed-Truesdale all rights reserved. No part of this book may be used or reproduced by any means, graphic, electronic, or mechanical, including photocopying, recording, taping or by any information storage retrieval system without the written permission of Jumpmaster Press™ and G.G. Garth, except in the case of brief quotations embodied in critical articles and reviews.

This book is a work of fiction. The characters, incidents, and dialogue are drawn from the author's imagination and are not to be construed as real. Any resemblance to actual events or persons, alive or dead, is entirely coincidental. Registered trademarks and service marks are the property of their respective owners.

Cover art copyright ©2021 Jumpmaster Press™
Library Cataloging Data
Names: G.G. Garth, Ghia Szwed-Truesdale
Title: Dragon Slayer of the Pink Salt Dead Sea Desert
5 in. × 8 in. (13.97 cm × 21.59 cm)
Description: Jumpmaster Press™ digital eBook edition | Jumpmaster Press™ Trade paperback edition | Alabama: Jumpmaster Press™, 2021. P.O Box 1774 Alabaster, AL 35007 info@jumpmasterpress.com
Summary: Dragon Slayer's mission to wipe out avian reptiles derails when he and the Genie of the Pink Sand Dead Sea Desert Oasis fall in love. When Genie, lamp, and magic carpet, Knotty, are kidnapped by the Vilest Crimson Dragon, the tiny Fairy Queen is their only hope of survival.

ISBN-13: 978-1-949184-88-4 (eBook) | 978-1-949184-45-7 (paperback)

1. Myths 2. Legends 3. Dragons 4. Magic Lamp 5. Fairies 6. Fairy Tale 7. Magic Realism

Printed in the United States of America

For more information: twitter.com/GGGarth; pph.me/GhiaWrite; https://www.facebook.com/ggarth1; GGGarthProductions.com

DRAGON SLAYER
OF THE PINK SAND DEAD SEA DESERT

G.G.GARTH

Coronial is an original hybrid term consisting of *Millennial*, *Colonial*, and *Corona*—as in the virus that trashed 2020. This hopeful adult fairy tale targets *Coronial* Readers. That is to say, Millennial Readers colonizing to survive in the time of Corona virus. The term *Coronial* was coined by Raffi Minasian specifically for G.G. Garth's post-Armageddon love story set far, far, *far* in the future—long after The Original Noah's Ark Flood, long after the Corona pandemic polyfecta, and long after the *next* flood, *The Most Recent Deluge*, as it will be termed, or *The Last Flood* in the following story.

For Slayer

Cyril!

Drop everything!

THIS RELIC WAS FOUND!

The Official & Historically-Accurate Saga of The Last Dragon Slayer

I want it in stores before the next wave hits!

Urgently, from your boss,
G.
The Publisher

PS Do not ignore this, Cyril! This one's *real*!

Real? Ha! My boss was so gullible. Given the number of times the tomb robber had barraged us with sham manuscripts, this one had to be a deep fake. Even so, I did take into consideration that until now, never had my boss, The Publisher, deployed exclamation marks with wanton abandon.

Her assistant, Niles, placed the note gingerly on my desk atop a stack of flaking parchment bound in a protective spider silk wrapper. As usual, Niles was wearing too much fake tan—*such a throwback!*

"Gone vintage, have you, Niles?" I joked.

Glowering inertly, Niles took the liberty of reminding me I was at risk of a pink slip.

I apologized and resisted underscoring that no one in the office believed he'd actually ever been *in* the sun, given its eclipse since *The Most Recent Deluge* back when the three black holes merged and took the sun with them.

"Newsflash, homie, tanning booths were outlawed centuries ago," I mewled smugly, not looking up from the *real* manuscript before me. "Nowadays, the only place you can see one of those cancer chambers is at the Science History Museum."

Niles grunted.

And anyway, I thought snidely, *since Earth remains lit by the fiery tail of the accretion of that black hole collision, there's no UV left worth basking in.*

"It's the melanin *They* put in the Vitamin D3 additive, Cyril," Niles shot back, defending his deep blood-orange hue. "*You* look like you could use some."

Fair enough, I thought. He'd invoked *They* as in the *They* to whom we were *all* subject. Our *Benevolent Overlords*. I backed off.

"You're so right, Niles." I allowed a taut, lippy smile to grace my coral lips. "*They* do put it in everything, don't *They*." Not seeking to embroil myself in one of those old fashioned Covid Era arguments, I withdrew, especially given that my cutaneous wrapper had been rendered a uniquely luminous orange at the very inception of my own blessed Petri Dish gestation.

"Don't patronize me, Cyril." Niles fled my office muttering flatly, "*Dissed by a Neon*."

I bragged crisply after him, "I can read in the dark, Niles!" I liked my neon benefits.

Down the hall, he released an impertinent snort as my attention returned to my boss' hand-written note in front of me. Mystery enshrouded this "*Historically Accurate*" account—*Real?* My boss said so. The tomb robber had kindly supplied a partial translation and a summary. And so, I read. And read. And I never stopped. Not until I reached the last page of the detailed summary. By then, several cycles of meteor showers had passed. So engrossed was I in this new manuscript that I did not even hear the bomb shelter alarms. My colleagues bunker-hunkered safely, while fallout from a *soulmates super nova* grazed the roof of our office pod. Yet I read on, oblivious to the molten gold blistering down my therma-glass windows and thudding inside the air shaft.

The more I read about *The Last Dragon Slayer of The Pink Salt Dead Sea Desert*, the more I was compelled to agree with my boss that we *should* publish it before the next wave hit. Even if the tomb raider had hocked us a deep fake, *this* one took me away from the hell we'd been living for decades. Yes, despite the sun's eclipse, we still had lunar rotations. And, yes, we kept count.

Found inside a *terra cotta* wine vessel deep inside an ancient dwarf mine, the parchment on which the Dragon Slayer's account was written radiocarbon dated to antediluvian times—we're going back *several* floods, mind you! So, I set forth to contract the anonymous purveyor—a slithery reptile of a grifter who'd oft pitched us *rare* manuscripts of spurious provenance. Until now, we'd not succumbed. Verification was essential.

Next, our big challenge lay in fact checking and footnoting the translation. Tough going as the language of the original manuscript appeared rooted in an ancient tongue related to Sumerian laced with elements of Sino-Tibetan, Aramaic, Cantabrigian, and *wicked-smaaaht* Bostonian. Many sections were indecipherable. We discovered that this was due to the elderberry ink having been smeared with another dark substance. Given who its seller was, I assumed Fenway ketchup. However, DNA tests revealed it to be a blood type unknown to any organism alive on earth since long before Darwin's last dodo *went south.*

What further confounded our forensics team was the narrative itself. The manuscript was written in three distinct hands. The majority of the ragged parchment sheets seemed to have been quilled by a local bard. We learned that she had been hired by the Chief Berber Medicine Man of an oasis surrounded by salty pink sand. As I came to understand the important pages I held in my hands, the *oeuvre's* overarching mission solidified. It chronicled the fall of the last dragons on earth—one by one—and exposed the fate of The Vilest Crimson Dragon.

Poignant, small notations found in the blood-soaked sidebar margin were sufficiently legible to reveal two voices—of lovers: a slayer of dragons named *Achilles* and a genie referred to solely as *Genie.* To corroborate our findings, we searched historic DNA imprints archived on the archaic *genealogy.com* and cross-referenced it against *23andme.* Then, we compared data to facts known to have appeared in *The Pink Salt Dead Sea Scrolls* that carbon-dated to the same time and to what appear to be the same two unique characters who appear in *carbondating.com,* the archive of famous ancient lovers. Who *were* these star-crossed lovers? Seems they were renowned in that era for their professional excellence. Achilles the Dragon Slayer was revered for... yes, his tacit skill. And Genie, it seems, was beloved for granting wishes to hapless strangers lost in the Pink Salt Dead Sea Desert. Its fearsome dunes were impassable between said oasis and the Mirage Mountains—lair to dragons and their protein source—the simple mountainfolk.

Additional research gave us to understand that, in fact, a Pink Salt Dead Sea Desert Oasis did once exist. It lay in a remote corner of what is now Armenia's capitol. Yerevan crouches at the base of Mount Ararat whose unreachable pinnacle is rumored to hold Noah's Ark glazed in ice, embedded in permafrost. There it has sat since the shores subsided after *The First Flood* deposited it there, millennia prior to *The Last Flood*—not to be confused with *The Most Recent Deluge* that took with it the Pink Salt Dead Sea Desert. With all our research, our Editorial staff puzzled affirmation with the forensics team. We concluded that a true account of these long-lost paramours *is* what we herewith avail.

A testament to following one's heart in times of greatest adversity, the lovers' story remains relevant today. Midst grit of salty pink sand and scalding dragon breath, this love blazed and flourished briefly. Though betrayed by external forces, the tale begins with the local Bard's catchy description of Achilles. When first read by our Editors, the bold image of said Dragon Slayer impelled our team to ignore cartons of Thai takeout, and remain lashed to our desks, unshaven until we cracked the code of our lucky literary find. E.g.:

...with pertinacious swagger, Slayer Achilles approached the dragon's nexus. Irrefutable

certainty smoldered in his gut—he knew his quarry was nigh. Once bitten by the beast, and thereby infected with its viral menace, Slayer was slowly dehydrating. Thus, too, however, Achilles alone had a sixth sense to detect from afar the green acid blood raging in the monster's veins as it quickened in fear at Our Hero's stealthy approach...

Who wouldn't fall for this capable man? Our entire Editorial team understood immediately why the wish-granting Genie fell in love with this fairy tale gent who—once upon a time—was as real and baronial as my own bioluminescent neon orange exterior. So, of course my bookworms and I had to get to the nucleus of Genie and Dragon Slayer Achilles' truth. *Imagine, I pondered, had they only known what a splash they would one day make on the social media scene in the post-ecliptic here and now... perhaps they'd have—what? Tried harder to survive? Eloped?*

Vanity Fair reports our best-seller is "a most sanguine saga spun for a lover." *Bloomberg* declared *Slayer* "the biggest blockbuster since naked Cleopatra wrapped herself in a Persian carpet and ordered the confection delivered like *DoorDash* to Julius Caesar." And *The New York Times Science Section*, after conducting its own radiography, infrared reflectography, and UV tests concurred that *Dragon Slayer* is "based on a true story." So, while this love story's veracity and origin *are* certain, the *denouement* of Slayer and Genie remains a mystery. One can only speculate whether evanescence prevailed, or—we hope—they got it together in the end. *You* be the judge.

—Cyril Neon, Editor

I

What on Earth Does Slayer Want?

Stealthy Dragon Slayer alighted from his vintage Corsair, in for repairs. Thick goggles shielded his steely eyes from biting bursts of salty pink sand. Looming thunderheads obscured searing mid-day sun. Rain slated steaming sands. Then a hot breath off the desert flipped Oasis leaves revealing pale green underbellies vulnerable to a quick fresh shot of lightning that cracked open the sky.

Ripping the desert air, the firebolt's charge set ions whirling like dervish dancers courting hope for exquisite trouble that lay ahead for the Dragon Slayer. Thunder clapped. Wind spat, clearing the heavy air of The Pink Salt Dead Sea Desert Oasis.

Our Hero crossed the landing strip, hailed by Oasis citizens—devotees, acolytes, and wanna-be dragon slayers brandishing inferior arms of ill-hewn brass or brittle desert tin. His torn Achilles sensed the storm's barometric shift. He limped slightly.

The sky tightened, gushing fat raindrops that pelted the crowd as the handsome devil strode past adoring fans. Magnanimous, Slayer waved and grinned rakishly. Maidens fainted into a collective heap as if on cue. In fact, their loss of composure was entirely unrehearsed.

A spindly shirtless minion sweating in brocaded Loden green pants rushed forth bearing a heavy lead crystal decanter of iced *vin rosé*. Appreciatively, Our Hero quaffed and then patted the urchin on the head. By all reports, this jaw-dropping heartthrob was known to render a cardiac in many a *fallen* lass. Yet deep down, Slayer was humble, honest, and... as this tale shall reveal, soon to encounter a secret for which, it turns out, he longed.

Endearingly modest, Slayer lingered a moment to thank the crowd for their kind support. Then, *ONWARD!*

Like all antediluvian humans born without pockets to put a dime in, Slayer thrived, nevertheless, thanks to his worst foes. Dragons. Decimation of dragons enriched him with one king's ransom after another. In the entire Pink Salt Dead Sea Desert Kingdom, *née* in the world, the one and only famously-effective Dragon Slayer had but one singular goal today. One thought from which no impassioned fan, no delectable iced *rosé*, no moonlit bubble bath replete with fainting candle-lit maidens, could derail Our Hero's focus—*finish off the last of the dragons*. Our venerated Hero was resolute.

Yet, was that Slayer's *Life Wish*?

Slay Dragons: Action Verb

No, *no*, slaying dragons was *not* Slayer's singular *Life Wish*. But right this red hot minute, he was on a mission to wipe out the reptilian-avian menace. His *Life Wish* had to wait.

En route to secure a local thoroughbred, Achilles paused outside the walls of the Oasis. Across the pink salt sands, he gazed in the direction of the remote Mirage Mountains. To reach the dragon's lair covertly, he needed a most puissant steed. Refreshed as he was by the quaff of *rosé* and abating squall of desert rain, Our Hero felt ready. The cheering crowd drowned out the sound of beating wings. Not dragon wings—not yet. Slayer was caught off guard when suddenly he got swept up by a tornado of winged changelings—frail tiny gnats who together touted the strength of a Titan. High into the air the fairies billowed, ferrying Achilles up and up and over the white-washed barricade surrounding the ancient Pink Salt Dead Sea Desert Oasis.

Presently, the fairies deposited him within the resilient fortress walls. In the oasis courtyard, the fairies left him coughing on a glittery cloud of magic dust that liquefied in his dry throat like honey. As the diminutive beauties darted away he was reminded of dragon flies and hummingbirds. They giggled and sang resonant as one billion sterling silver bells, while at Slayer Achilles, they blew kisses whose fervent sting tingled his countenance.

Within the open market, a crowd gathered to catch flecks of the precious sparkling fairy dust. Bewildered by the lush abundance he beheld within the oasis walls, Dragon Slayer stood astonished. He was surrounded by every imaginable artful thing he had ever dreamed of, and hundreds he never even knew existed. Everything beautiful in the world was *here. Everything EXCEPT* for the *ONE* secret *thing* Slayer had wanted all his life—that *Life Wish* thing. And that one secret thing he had most wanted all his life had *pas* to do with his formidable skill at slaying dragons for a living—or so he believed.

Was it the thunderclouds scudding across the afternoon sky? It seemed to Our Hero that the light there inside The Pink Salt Dead Sea Desert Oasis walls was mystically misty. Dappled and dazzled in green and gold, sapphire and fuchsia, with sparks of bronze, silver, and copper, the fountains, public art works and gorgeous graffiti, people and architecture, all caused Slayer to catch his breath in wonder.

"Pulchritudinous," mused Slayer.

And then it began.

The crowd parted to make way for the Oasis' choreographed welcome party bearing delights. The first order of delight to emerge from the veritable bouquet of silk-clad dervish waiters was an extinct-mahogany tray bearing comestible treats and iced *rosé* in the finest sharp-cut stemware.

"Baccarat," Slayer guessed. Drawing the substantial glass to his parched lips, it was with gratitude that Our Hero savored long cooling *gorgées*.

When the second order of delight was bestowed, it was whirled into place beneath his backside by two dervishes in raw orange silk. A *recamier* of tender peach lambskin like none Slayer had ever touched. On it he reclined most comfortably under a palm frond lofted by a curiously-attentive eunuch with a gap between his front teeth flanked frightfully by stabby-looking incisors.

After Slayer's hair-raising (and hair-razing!) flight across the pink, salty sands of time for the purpose of extirpating dragons, Slayer was thankful for a brief reprieve. *I must restore myself while I await the delivery of my rental thoroughbred.* An Oasis steed alone, he believed, was sufficiently *au fait* to transport him into the bowels of the dragon's lair.

Then came the third order of delight—for good things come in three's, and Pythagoras had an algorithm to prove it. A larger-than-life laughing Genie approached toting a small burnished brass oil lamp. The Genie wore an ill-fitting velvet vest of pink to match the glorious pink of the Pink Salt Dead Sea Desert. A bright green patchwork tunic, furthermore, covered naught of the Genie's bulging belt band above black silk pantaloons. *Crunches*, thought Slayer, *are unknown to this dude*. Disconcerting as it was for Slayer to observe Genie's mass of equal height and width, he zipped his thoughts hermetically. *The Genie's so gargantuan. How's it possible?* As Slayer looked for the outer edges of Genie's silhouette, he marveled at nature's ability to store energy, like a battery, in adipose tissue.

It was a well-known *true fact* based on *real news* that *The Last Flood* had washed away all who could not outrun its great tsunami—not unlike the quarry orangutan after fruit masting season, ravaged readily by the clouded leopard. Yet, there stood Genie, larger than life, grinning ear-to-ear at the Dragon Slayer. Achilles simply could not wrap his mind around the breadth of girth before him. And given the acute angle of the brilliantly setting sun, nor could he rightly discern Genie's outline without staring obviously and therefore rudely. Our Hero averted his eyes. He was quintessentially discrete and far too polite to inquire after a detail that might well have just been an inconceivable personal health choice on the part of the Genie. *Don't let this happen to you*, Slayer Achilles thought wryly of gifting a lettered t-shirt to his new acquaintance, then spanked away the unkind thought with a fond memory of the Wildfit curriculum. *Dude just needs a bro to workout with*, thought Slayer.

Achilles was forced to stop hyper-focusing on the Genie's utter lack of sports-fitness when the Genie leaned in. Too close.

Piquant propinquity, thought Slayer, retreating marginally.

"Guess what, Dragon Slayer!" whispered the Genie with an infectious grin not unlike that of Our Hero.

And in that very moment the two strangers bonded as they broke into inexplicable peals of laughter. They laughed for a reason apparent neither to themselves nor to the on-looking dervishes and residents of The Pink Sand Dead Sea Desert Oasis.

"I get three wishes?!" Dragon Slayer's ragged breath caught between a lingering string of chuckles. "Right, Genie?!"

"Nnnnnope!" Genie laughed.

"What?! No wishes?!" exclaimed Our Hero in disbelief. "But what about, '*rub the lamp, make three—*.'"

"You get *ONE* wish, Slayer."

"One..." Slayer's brow furrowed.

"Choose wisely."

"Man, this deal's fraught with conditions." Our canny Hero was dismayed for the duration of one Planck unit of time—*that*, incidentally, is less than a nanosecond.

Genie winked and purred, "*Meh*, no conditions... not *really*. Except... well, it takes time for your wish to steep, like—"

"Like tea," Slayer finished Genie's sentence. Again they giggled.

"Yes, a wish is like a well-brewed tea," Genie confirmed. "Only after four days at The Oasis will your wish materialize."

"But, I've got dragons to slay, Genie."

"Trust me, Slayer—four days of rest. Those inflammatory buzzards will still be there."

"But—"

"Rules!"

Slayer sighed.

"So? What's your wish?"

"Interesting question, Genie." Slayer stalled, not really believing he could have what he truly wanted by simply wishing on a brass lamp in the hands of some guy in serious need of a pre-emptive coronary biohack.

"I bet the answer's much more interesting than the question," crooned Genie, stroking the small lamp contemplatively.

Ignoring the sagacious Genie for a moment, Slayer smirked and chucked a munificent wink at a cute girl ogling him from the crowd. Thereupon—overcome by bliss—the fecund lass fainted and had to be lugged off to the infirmary by eunuchs. Before Slayer spoke again, the Genie seemed to read his mind.

"No wishing for extra wishes, Slayer."

Again, the two fell into resplendent peals of laughter that cascaded into a ripple of giggles among the villagers.

"Wait! So..." A residual chuckle escaped Slayer's lips. "*Can* I slay dragons during this *steeping* period?" Eager to complete the job for which he had flown his Corsair across the desert—and rack up yet another king's ransom from foiled dragon spoils—Slayer waited politely for Genie to answer.

"Sure, Slayer." Genie shrugged. "You can slay dragons anytime. And you can bolt to the Mirage Mountains the moment your Arabian steed is delivered. The stable boy shall see to it. Meanwhile..." Genie smirked mischievously and palmed a wad of *baksheesh* to the scrawny groom in the Loden green brocaded trousers. "Our young ostler here will check the stables to arrange your thoroughbred. And... since you're new in town, Slayer, I'm in charge of showing you what The Oasis has to offer."

"Will that be all, Genie?" asked the young lad.

Genie took the urchin aside. "Kid," whispered the Genie, "make yourself scarce. And, *uhhm*, hobble that horse 'til *I* call for it."

"You want me to—"

"No, don't actually hurt the horse," whispered Genie, "Just don't have it ready to go for four days."

Dispatched by the Genie, the ostler nodded and ran off with a fistful of graft. Adjusting a tunic cuff, Genie returned to Slayer's side.

"What's up your sleeve, Genie?" Achilles was ready to make his wish, and grab grub.

"Oh, it's a surprise," was Genie's deadpan reply. "You'll have to wear a blindfold."

Slayer liked surprises. He never tired of trying what he had not yet done. Given he had traveled widely to undo many a dragon, he'd *seen-it-done-it-been-there*. And he so relished the possibility that an actual Genie had the ability to show him what he had never experienced.

"What'll we do first, Genie? After I make my wish, that is."

"Much to see and experience within the walls of The Oasis!" assured the Genie, and handed Slayer another iced *rosé* despite the nagging worry of over-serving him alcohol, and risking dehydration especially in that intense desert heat.

"Great, I'm all yours, Genie."

Genie liked the sound of *that* and smiled broadly. A pudgy hand waggled the brass lamp. "Ready to make your wish, Slayer?"

"Born ready." Slayer considered his one secret *Life Wish*. He'd never told anyone. "*Ummmm*, Genie, might I hold onto your lamp?" hazarded Slayer, reaching for the burnished vessel. "Just 'til my wish comes true."

"Fat chance!" *No lamp, no leverage!* thought Genie and laughed, suspiciously covetous of the magic ewer clasped 'twixt hands as big as bear paws. "C'mon, hurry up and make your wish, Slayer, so we can go carouse!"

And so, mesmerized, Genie searched Slayer's face as he closed his dreamy brown eyes to rub *la lampe magique*. From it, a voltaic charge effervesced as the slayer of dragons wished the *One Wish* that gnawed his heart like a chew-toy since, well, since as far back as he could recall. The crowd shied in awe when magic swirled in vast arabesques from Slayer's muscular hand where it lingered on the little lamp—held stubbornly by the Genie. Gloaming brightened faces of onlookers, as a cat-canary smirk graced the Genie's lips. And there we leave for all to *wonder-in-slumber* what the Dragon Slayer wanted so ardently for his one *Life Wish.*

Dragon Slayer

During the coming days, while Slayer's *One Wish* was steeping like a bespoke English blend in The Great Brown Tea Pot of the Universe, Genie got Slayer's Corsair serviced. The mechanic was none other than Phil K., whom everyone called *Filk*. Luckily for Slayer Achilles, *Filk* was an acclaimed monk-in-residence who authored *Zen & the Art of Corsair Maintenance*. After a visit to the repair hangar, the large miracle-worker set about to arrange for myriad earthly delights on Our Hero's blindfolded behalf. Genie squired Slayer from scenic vista to scenic vista—each time tying and untying his pink silk blindfold.

"...Ta-da! The sixth wonder of The Oasis... Ta-da! The seventh wonder of The Oasis..."

The glorious surprises were interspersed with frequent barhopping. *Why, but to delight him*, thought Genie smiling ever more—perhaps too wistfully. Initially, Genie was helpful like this just *because*. It was the right thing to do. Slayer was new. And Genie had been raised to welcome guests with great fanfare. So, as the two new associates explored and ate and sipped at every venue the Oasis had to offer, friendship's seedling sprouted.

Genie enjoyed watching the maidens faint over gallant Slayer—*live entertainment!* Reciprocally, Slayer had determined the Genie to be affable with a wicked sense of fun—*a kindred spirit*, thought Slayer. Apart from the curveball chemistry Genie felt for Achilles, another reason to hang around with him soon percolated up from the sub-stratum of Genie's mind. If Achilles was as capable a dragon slayer as his *éclat* foretold, then, ostensibly, he could facilitate Genie's one clandestine wish.

Unlike every other wish on the planet, Genie's alone could not be fulfilled by the magic lamp. Though spawned by a compromising secret related *to* the magic lamp, Genie's *compromise* was dragon-*spawned*. Incurred by one particular dragon, in fact. *The Vilest Crimson Dragon*. It was not a nice dragon. Not that any of them were. But *this* one had spellbound Genie with neither a kind nor an honorable spell. So, every day, the Genie obsessed about how to get free. And since the Oasis villagers had learned of the renowned dragon slayer whose goal it was to wipe out every last flying *torchier* on earth, many an invitation had been issued to Slayer. Finally, Achilles had accepted. When the Bard announced that Slayer Achilles would soon make a pit stop at the Oasis, citizens celebrated, and prepared to welcome him grandly. Genie, however, had secretly recited incantations, praying that this *real-deal* dragon slayer would be the one, once and for all, to man-up and free the Genie from The Curse of The Vilest Crimson Dragon.

More on that shall be disclosed in due course. For now, Genie removed Achilles' raw silk blindfold, and he found himself in a crush of barefoot belly dancers inside *The Harem Bar & Grill*. They sallied through the crowd and past the buffet.

"Say, Slayer?" probed Genie whose feigned nonchalance jousted eagerness. "You claim you're after dragons, *eh*? Any *one* in particular?"

As the two unexpected friends bellied up to the bar, a devil-may-care twinkle sparked across Achilles' rugged mien. "Well, Genie, I'll take down any dragon I can find 'til I deracinate the lot of'em," he replied puckishly, wagging four fingers at the barkeep. "My good man, 100% agave, please. Red worm in each."

"Brace yourself."

The barroom mushroomed with veiled dancers who gave the impression of jellyfish undulating in a sea of hunched eunuchs in ossified linen that matched the pallor of their skin. Achilles was swiftly jostled by the crowd onto a *recamier*, and Genie followed. Sitar music emanated from opulent Persian carpets that twanged and sang whilst luxuriating across the floors throughout the spacious establishment. Genie complimented their plush luster.

"Take your shoes off, Genie!" shrieked one especially lovely silk carpet in hues of blue, green, purple, and saffron. "Damned points on your heels are killing us."

"Sorry, dudes," replied the Genie relinquishing a pair of sharp-heeled curl-toed slippers with which a dervish whirled away to the shoe rack by the entry.

Content, Slayer smiled as he raised two shots of mezcal to examine a red worm in each.

Observing Achilles, Genie thought twice, wondering, *Am I an enabler?*

Without skipping a beat, however, they downed the piquant libation and its rubicund contents.

"Why dragons...?" asked Genie diffidently, "...as opposed to, say, Leviathans?"

"Dragons're my *thing*." Slayer smiled in a way that lit up the entire *Harem Bar*.

Equally disconcerted, Genie experienced a jarring loss of focus on all but Slayer's lambent grin. "Tell me more," stuttered Genie abashed and downright stupefied at having been blinded by Slayer's irrepressible charm. Normally, Genie disdained pretty much everyone. At best, Genie was indifferent to the brio of legion oasis visitors whose wayward wishes were to be granted by the sole custodian of the brass lamp.

"Dragon-slaying's what I do for a living, Genie. *Niche market!*" Unassuming, Slayer leaned back and chucked down another shot. "I excelled at an early age. Stuck with it."

Faltering, Genie took a moment to sip, mesmerized as Slayer picked the red worm from his teeth and chewed it before swallowing. Genie soldiered on, "Is it what you wanna be doing when you're, like, 85?"

Slayer thought long and hard before replying, "Insurance liabilities *are* steep. But I've got many bankable decades of shelf-life left in me. *More* with all the replacement parts available nowadays."

"Clearly *you* don't need replacement parts, Slayer, I mean just look at you, you…" Genie choked on the words, "…*you're…perf—*" Stopping short of blurting, "*You're perfect for me!*" Genie blushed, adjusted the folds that comprised the sorcerer's mass, and to which Our Hero politely turned a blonde-eye. Recovering, Genie affirmed artfully, "You're, *uhhmm*, perfectly *healthy*, Achilles."

"My torn Achilles heel hurts sometimes," confessed Achilles modestly. *Ah, so he wasn't perfect!* Oblivious to Genie's *perfect* discombobulation, Slayer continued, "Think of it this way, Genie. Stats show that only four score and seven dragons remain on earth to challenge me." Genie nodded knowingly and gazed at his lips as he spoke. "And, Genie, each of these giant winged lizards is nested on a belated king's ransom! *Payola pour moi, baby!* Plus, it's fun."

"Cool," murmured Genie suppressing the urge to plant a big fat smooch right smack on Our Hero's bewitching smile. Instead, Genie knocked back a shooter and hailed a triple round, thus obviating entirely any lingering concerns of guilt, gout, consumption, *or* dipsomania.

"*Niche market!*" exclaimed Genie and Slayer in tandem and they tripped into a giggle fit at the synchronicity of their silly outburst. The two unlikely associates *chin-chinned* their freshened vials, each replete with a red Mexican moth caterpillar pickled in fermented agave. Tossing back another scorcher, both friends marveled that, quite off-the-cuff, they had spoken the same random phrase, shouted it out, *together*. After scant longer than a nanosecond of carousing, decadence, and inebriation, the accidental allies had fallen to finishing each other's thoughts.

Halfway to the Slayer's Wish-Fulfilment Day, the adventitious couple of pub-crawlers showed no signs of party fatigue. Slayer seemed utterly contented. Although he did, *er,* rather frequently leap up to brandish his sword and demonstrate his agility when it came to sticking a dragon at a perspicacious angle. Genie, in contrast, ignored pangs of culpability that all this partying might weaken the Slayer's chance of out-maneuvering the worst dragon of them all. Genie just sat there, immobile on a barstool, slightly stewed. Genie was especially grateful to have encountered an equal of good cheer who was a blast to hang around with—a man's man, a real man who took no prisoners. Genie just needed to do a great big 'note-to-self' to chill and focus on business. For each time the Dragon Slayer smiled or sat close at hand it caused the Genie to stutter or altogether forget entire blocks of thought.

Grinning happily, Achilles glanced over. "So Genie, seems we visited all the museums, markets, and bars here in the Salty *Sink Pand* Oasis of *theformerDeadSea,*" Slayer slurred.

"*Sssssink Pand!?*" Genie slurred back through riotous laughter accompanied by a red worm projectile that struck a belly dancer in the navel. "Oooops. Sorry!"

"What *elseistheretosee* in *thismagicalplace*?" Slayer's gaze melted Genie's aching heart.

Not bored, *per se*, but Slayer was itching to perambulate his appreciable muscles off the tender peach lambskin *recamier* upon which he lay. He itched to run around. He itched to break a sweat. Maybe scale a cliff or deep sea dive to get his blood circulating and oxygenate his brain. Sensing those were not activities Genie would do easily, Slayer elected not to body-shame his new friend. And instead, he sat happily sipping Macallan's neat to which they switched evenings when the desert swelter shed itself down to shiver digits.

Even as the belly dancers performed before him—frond-fanned as he was, again, by the officious gap-toothed eunuch—Slayer longed to do strategic maneuvers. He needed to get a bird's-eye of dragon-lair-land that lay across The Pink Salt Dead Sea Desert. As if reading Slayer's mind, Genie leaned in close and suggested two solutions: a solution to Slayer's need to get a tactical overview of his quarry's terrain, and, another dram of Macallan's.

"*Citadel Bar and Grill* in the Central Garden," whispered Genie with *perplexing propinquity*. "From up there, we can scout dragon flight patterns! Killer mint juleps, too!"

"I'm all in!" exclaimed Slayer with the very grin that shut down Genie's frontal cortex, causing this otherwise competent magical adult to stammer helplessly.

"Bit of a hike though, Slayer, we'll need m-m-my m-m-magic carpet, Knotty... that's its name, not *naughty*... but *Knot*—" Genie decided to shut the hell up and demonstrate to Slayer how to unfurl a magic carpet. "Come, Knotty!"

Forthwith, Knotty appeared at Genie's side, flipped itself about in the air, then leveled out. Awaiting orders, Knotty hovered and flirted with the sweet silken Persian who had complained of Genie's sharp shoes.

Genie leaned in closer to Slayer and whispered, "Hop on."

Chafing at Genie's closing of the polite social distancing gap between them, Slayer sprang to his feet. "Race you, Genie!" Slayer glanced back, grinning, thus sparing Genie mortification as he recoiled from his companion. "To the *Citadel*!"

At that very moment, a grave rumbling shook every drink in the house. Ominous clinking of glass silenced guests. Dervishes ceased whirling. Harem girls' clanging bells snuffed. Knotty dropped to the floor to protect Silky. Eunuchs, bartenders, everyone *hit the deck!*

"Dragon incoming!" trilled the turbaned doorman before he went up in a crisp of smoke along with all the shoes in the shoe rack.

Dragon Slayer

4

A pall of malodorous dragon breath engulfed *The Harem Bar* as a hoary blue monstrosity snorted and scraped at the windows of the thatch and mud whitewashed structure.

"It's the dreaded Cerulean Blue Dragon!" wheezed Genie. "Be careful, Slayer."

Terrified, Genie glanced up from a puddle of sweaty enormity to witness Slayer grinning broadly. He stared down the dragon whose giant veined eyeball peered in through the charred doorway. Slayer stood his ground—unlike the eunuchs, dervishes, belly dancers, bartender, and Genie. All remained prone upon the floor, gasping in fear. Stealthily, Our Hero drew his glinting platinum blade.

"I'm sorry, Slayer," whimpered Genie clutching the magic lamp. "Sorry, I can't help you with m-m-m-magic. M-m-m-my powers are restricted to an eternity of granting strangers' wishes." And everyone else in the bar had already used up their wish.

It was then Genie heard the words that alchemized relief and trust in the very heart of our dear prestidigitator. "No worries, Genie, *I've got your back!*" Slayer reassured his friend.

For a moment, Achilles detected a pinkish rend in Genie's plumber's-back. He glanced again. *Or, perhaps it was just another 'battery pack' of excess adipose tissue? Now's not the time to analyze the incongruity of Genie's vast stores of energy*, Slayer decided. At last, he had a dragon to slay. And, man, it was big, and it was blue, and so...

Our Hero crept out the back...

...and around to the front.

Slayer Achilles lay low until he reached the hind quarters of the unsuspecting, stinking, Cerulean Blue Dragon... whom Our Hero readily and, *sans* any particular stratagem or drama, slew. In three deft swipes—for more power comes in three's—Slayer eviscerated the Cerulean Blue Dragon. Upon removing its gushing entrails, he tied its intestines around the dragon's wings, limbs, and mouth to avoid a post-mortem fireblast.

"Done!" Dragon Slayer announced placidly, "At ease, Oasis Citizens!"

Before their eyes, the blue behemoth died a quick, humane death. Everyone cheered. Thereupon, Slayer declared his intention to share the dragon's immense treasure with the citizens of The Oasis. Although some offered Sherpa services, it is worth noting that the Oasis citizens did not need the treasure because already they had absolutely everything you could possibly imagine. Yet, graciously they accepted Slayer's *noblesse oblige*. Their discrete intention was to later re-gift the rainbow of gemstones and gold bullion to hapless travelers: Travelers lost and wandering in the interminably vast pink salt desert outside The Oasis' walls that separated that lovely place from marauder and miscreant alike. But alas, neither the hellish eternity of searing pink salt sand nor even the highest wall could shield Oasis citizens from dragons.

Spontaneously then at *The Harem Bar*, an improv kegger ensued whereby Slayer was *fêted* for slaying the Cerulean Blue Dragon. The hallowed Oasis Bard, forced from retirement, grudgingly composed a ballad extolling Our Hero's stealth and prowess [its rough translation seems to belie a monotonous, even ominous, somewhat Germanic—albeit marginally ridiculous—Gregorian chant type feel]:

The Cerulean Blue Dragon's magnitude,
while formidable
is naught compared to the red one.
—caveat emptor—
The blue dragon was no match
for The Vilest
Crimson Dragon.
This beast terrorizes oasis dwellers,
nomads, and mountain folk...
Deus ex machinaaaaaa,
Aaaaaaaaaamennnnnnnnn.

Sotto voce, with measured determination and a spit-gob of disdain, Genie muttered, though not a soul heard, "The Vilest Crimson Dragon shackled me... I pray, not much longer."

Bubbly toasts flowed as the Bard's ballad to the mastery of Achilles wrapped up and harem girls offered—some even *begged!*—to bear his proverbial seed to create a nation of dragon slayers. Genie scowled, ordering the dazzling dancers to *piss right off!*—and added abruptly, "There shall be no belly-dancing dragon slayers spawned on my watch."

One beauteous muse after another: Slayer, nonplussed, declined politely. He wanted to risk neither a health hazard for himself, nor to incur damsel-offense. Nor wished he render himself redundant. Given that he had zero competition, he rejected the idea of an entire crop of Alpha-challenging slayers. He intended, for decades to come, to retain his current position with unfettered access to historic treasure troves wherever dragons nested. Furthermore, he was *biologically complete* with a very fine daughter and a very fine son residing safely and happily in a place far from dragons that was reachable only by Corsair.

As the party din grew louder, whirling dervishes, like inverted calla lilies, spun in stiff white dresses with fanning skirts. Dejected belly dancers nevertheless did what belly dancers do best, set to sterling silver and tin bells accompanied by a serious *one-two* down beat on the kidskin tympanum.

Fanning palm fronds to the beat, a coterie of eunuchs looked on.

Genie pulled up a silken ottoman alongside Our Hero. Perplexed, Slayer noticed with some trepidation that Genie again settled in beside him just a micron closer than what might otherwise be considered socially appropriate despite their friendship.

"*Not* too late for last call at *Citadel Bar & Grill*," coaxed Genie whose voice seemed to Slayer softer than usual, even uncomfortably vulnerable. That gave Slayer a curious warm feeling. Ultimately, he wrote it off as a mere dopamine rush from battle fatigue—having just slain the Cerulean Blue Dragon. Still, the curious comforting moment gave Slayer pause. Genie was, after all, clearly a guy. *Right?* That was obvious to everyone! Not to mention incomprehensibly disinterested in Slayer's fitness regimen! *Not that there's anything wrong with that!* Slayer self-corrected as his own politically-astute internal-editor hastened to chasten the natural-born athlete.

"To the Citadel then, Genie!" Slayer concurred.

"We'll observe the night flight patterns of The Vilest Crimson Dragon."

"*That's* my next quarry!"

"Oh, *really*?" Genie purred smiling deep inside. "And, why's that?"

Slayer was keen to get outside—fresh night air and a walk with his friend, away from the tintinnabulation of *The Harem Bar* party. Plus, the pallid eunuchs kept migrating too closely and creeping him out. Slayer liked his space.

"Well, Genie," replied Slayer, stepping aside for his friend to pass barefoot through the charred doorway, "I figure if I take out the vilest of them all, it'll scare the other dragons into submission. They'll be easier to nail."

"Cool! You'll love the *Citadel*!" Genie worried that the words came out too eagerly. "It's spectacular watching dragons' distant flashes fire-balling the night sky! Like fireflies' fireworks."

"Fireflies' fireworks, works for me," said Slayer enthusiastically, "But I bet they're..."

"...*way bigger*!" They both said *way bigger* at the same time. And, instead of *LTAO* like they normally did, Genie and Slayer went chalk-silent and blushed when they glanced into one another's eyes. Finally both of them broke, blurting gleefully, "*The Citadel! Race you!*"

Amidst peals of laughter the race was on.

Day 3 at The Pink Sand Dead Sea Desert Oasis

It was one day before Slayer's Wish Fulfilment Day and the desert heat was oppressive. Our Hero, the Dragon Slayer, awoke shortly past sunrise to a red sky. Only then he discovered himself in a crumpled heap above the skyline on dew-damp stones under a blistering ball of desert fire.

Genie? Where's—? What the heck happened? Reeling, Slayer tried to shake off the swoony effects of Macallan's followed by myriad mint juleps he and Genie had downed after his Cerulean Blue Dragon slaying party. That coupled with champagne chasing down red worms marinated in aged agave and—a slammer headache rivaled abashed befuddlement.

Where am I? Dazed atop *The Citadel*, Our Hero rubbed his beard bristles and glanced 'round to identify his whereabouts. Apart from a penguin-dressed waiter who lay snoring peacefully in a far corner of the stone patio near the bar, Slayer was alone at *The Citadel*. The southpaw rubbed his sinistral sword arm; every one of his sinewy muscles ached.

Where the heck is Genie?

The previous night started to come back to him in shards of Macallan's flotsam and mint julep jetsam—and then, for a skinny-minute, his mental acuity cleared.

"Oh *gawd*," Slayer whispered. "What've I done!? Genie's a guy...! Or... is he a...?"

The Kink's *Lola* echoed in the dungeons of his temporal lobe. Slayer could only vaguely recall and he wasn't quite sure if what he suspected he had experienced with Genie was real. And he really needed to find Genie to confirm what the heck had *gone down*... between them. He wanted to be sure they were still friends, if an, *er*, indiscretion or calamitous impropriety had spontaneously combusted under the influence of juleps, *et. al.*

Slayer sweated profusely, swallowing nausea.

It was coming back to him. After too many sloppy slush-puppies, there had been an interlude, a vibe, *uhhh*... alcohol miasma liquidated Slayer's memory. Chagrin gnawed his very bones from within and he bowed his head. That hurt, too.

Oh Genie, We have to talk, he thought decidedly, *we'll figure it out*. He knew he'd have to take the lead on this one with his quixotic co-conspirator.

"Genie?" Slayer called out to the desert breeze.
Nada.

His head throbbed. His Achilles ached. He remembered: *Red* and *Dragon*.

"Oh, crapulence," he muttered, lumbering to his feet. "Crapadina!" He noticed recent raw wounds on his arms. *How'd I...?*

Slayer leaned his taut abs against the crumbly crenellation encircling *The Citadel* and looked out. In the distance, happy oasis merchants had begun to set up shop in the open market. Far beyond, on the horizon, sulfurous smoke rose in thin tendrils... from the cave of The Vilest Crimson Dragon as it slept off last night's brush with Slayer-inflicted death. Endeavoring to heal its own wounds, the alary monstrosity had stuffed the slashes and gashes inflicted by Our Hero with antibacterial gold bullion cached to the stalactite ceiling of its lair. Prescient as a blood brother, Slayer Achilles sensed his nemesis' thoughts as it dreamt of last night's skirmish.

"I coulda' had you, flying rat-bastard!" Slayer shouted in the direction of The Vilest Crimson Dragon far away under the distant mountains. "Next time, it's a take-down! A single-stroke!" *Tonight!*

But what had happened with Genie?

Head in hands.

Cobwebs.

Slayer did recall that he and Genie had raced to the *Citadel Bar*. Squarely, slowly, he pieced it together: Achilles himself and his healing Achilles heel had got infused with a good hit of endorphins while racing on foot alongside Genie on Knotty that stunning 100-knots-per-square-inch silk and wool blend adorned with fractal arabesques. Magic of course, for how else could the colossus that was the

Genie transit 1000 spiral steps to the top of *The Citadel Bar & Grill* tower.

Even though Genie summarily beat him to the pinnacle of *The Citadel*, Slayer had gleefully climbed up the endless caracole of steps, generously feeding his rock-hard calves and quads with a femoral infusion. Way at the top of the tower, by the crenellation, the two friends had sat enjoying Chesapeake blue crab cakes, oysters dashed with limed horseradish, truffle fries, and way too many syrupy cocktails. All the while, they watched the distant horizon where dragons blazed about in nocturnal terrorization of the diffident but delicious mountain villagers.

Slayer recalled more. For sure, they'd sauced the night away, and, for sure, barriers had, *uhmmm*, dropped, as it were. And then *two* more odd *things* had happened simultaneously. Both confounded Slayer. But, one of which still *confounded* Slayer most especially.

The First Confounding Thing was less confounding than *The Second Confounding Thing*. Yet it was still bloody confounding. It was this:

The Vilest Crimson Dragon had swept in unexpectedly alighting on *The Citadel*, inciting mayhem. Guests who fled down the spiral stone staircase were briskly torched. Others hid behind the bar with the waiter. Thereupon Slayer stuck the crusty intruder. Several times his glistening platinum blade sank to its hilt, drawing buckets of green acid blood that ate away a section of the stone crown wall of the tower.

But before Our Hero could plunge a deathblow into the leathery nethers of The Vilest Crimson Dragon, Slayer had become distracted. What distracted him? It was *The Second Confounding Thing*—a *thing* that he still could not quite rightly account for. *The Second Confounding Thing* had distracted Achilles from slaying the thorny red devil once and for all. And still now, even as he stretched his herculean forearms and squinted into the stabbing rays of morning sunlight, Slayer's mind could not fathom that *Second Thing* that he was certain he had witnessed in the night.

The Vilest Crimson Dragon had attacked Genie. *That was bad, of course!* As the red dragon sank its razor claws into Genie's copious folds, Slayer had flung himself between predator and prey—striking mercilessly at the creature. His sole goal was to save his dear friend, Genie. And then, out of the corner of his eye in a crevice of peripheral vision, *The Second Confounding Thing* had transpired:

Genie changed! No, not the pink and green outfit with black pantaloons! *Physically* changed! Shape-shifted.

But that's impossible! Did I hallucinate from the Mexican red worm? It was only for a fleeting *slow-mo-moment*; nevertheless it was a pulchritudinous moment that had mesmerized Slayer. *What did I see?* His besotted daze was short-lived—longer than a Planck, yet shorter than a millisecond. The equivocally mystifying distraction had lasted just long enough for The Vilest Crimson Dragon to escape. And with it, the stinking gargoyle ripped Genie from Slayer's grasp. Despite Genie's great mass, the powerful dragon flew off into the impenetrable obsidian night with Genie screaming in pain against embedded dragon talons.

Crushed by the loss of his friend, nonetheless, Slayer was certain, like a waking dream, he was 99.999% sure that he saw Genie change into... *Could it have been...?!* Slayer admonished his own hopes. Was *he* a... *she?* His heart was affected; it would be some time before he realized the true effect. Slayer would have gone after Genie right then under the mocking stars, but he'd blacked out from having drunk too much booze.

Hours later, in the searing morning sun on the stone deck of *The Citadel*, Slayer was overcome by grief and waves of nausea. Last night's excessive alcohol consumption consumed him as he threw up over the friable crenellation. "*Braaaaaack!*"

Then... *Splat*—Achilles succumbed to a face-plant on the granite slab floor, pancaked in another stone-cold blackout.

And so, for the remainder of Day Three at The Oasis, the otherwise valiant slayer of dragons lay useless. *Who knew* where Genie was? Bleak turned bleaker, despite the fretting Bard's assiduous efforts to revive Our Hero. First the harem girls were brought up to dance at their most alluring. "Unveiled to no avail," mourned the despondent Bard jealously ogling their undulations. Then dervishes alighted, spinning and quailing divine incantations from the poetry of Rumi. Also moot. Even the eunuchs gathered 'round to inspect the slumbering Slayer. Yet they reached him not a whit with their fragrant tinctures and reflexology.

At long last, as a desperate measure, the band of giggling winged changelings was asked, ever so politely, to make an appearance. This would cost The Oasis a tidy sum of its gemstone cache reserved for hapless desert wanderers, for the diaphanous fairies simply had never been bridled by anyone's wish. Not even when it came to reviving *the* Dragon Slayer. And while the silly winged sylphs were not greedy, in fact they were excessively kind, they did want to be reassured that The Oasis citizens appreciated and respected them. And what better for delicate fluttering beings than a portable form of energy such as gemstones. Riches that even the minutest among them could crush in her powerful jaws and convert into magic fairy dust.

"Tell jokes, tickle him!" the harried Bard pleaded, wringing her gnarled knuckles as she knelt solicitously before the glittering thoroughbred Queen of the winged waifs. Queen Elizabeth was suspended by her iridescent chiffon wings in mid-air slightly above the Bard's visage. The Queen of the fairies regarded the Bard with some degree of pity before she spoke, her voice warm like a late-summer stream.

"Bard, this is a naughty Gordian knot that hangs like Damocles' Sword," Queen Elizabeth inadvertently mixed her metaphors. "Yet there's naught we can do for the Dragon Slayer Achilles." As the tiny Queen humming-birded in mid-air, sparks of fairy dust fell upon the Bard's imploring face causing her withered skin to rehydrate to a youthful mien. "The Dragon Slayer is unresponsive, even to me. What he needs is—"

"What, Queen Elizabeth, pray tell—?" Everyone spoke at once, begging the diminutive noble to tell what could save Our Hero.

"Stop interrupting me and I'll tell you!" declared the stately albeit miniscule powder keg. "We need the Genie for this one, for the Genie is the guardian of the Slayer's One Wish."

"Genie alone can fix this?" The Bard sought reassurance.

Queen Elizabeth nodded, though herself uncertain. She dispatched a search party, enlisting each and every good citizen of The Oasis to look high and low, for they did not know yet what Slayer knew—that the Genie had been kidnapped by The Vilest Crimson Dragon. And so, in all The Oasis—every venue was searched. And mind you, the Genie was impossible to overlook. Yet, of course, the Genie was nowhere to be found, for at that very moment Genie languished bitterly in The Vilest Crimson Dragon's lair.

"We are faced with a bit of a Rubik's Cube, I'm afraid," declared the tiny fairy Queen as she determined what to do next. There had to be a solution that did not involve libations. *But what?* She was about to alight with her tribe of willowy winged ones to search for Genie in the opera house and public library—a last ditch effort. But before she could crisp up her perky gossamer wings, the stertorous waiter awoke screaming hoarsely.

Dragon Slayer

7

Keening, the penguin-dressed waiter awoke in terror from a nightmare about dragons. "*I saw it all!!*"

First Blue then Red: Two attacks on The Oasis in one day had been too much for the fellow. 'Til now 'midst mayhem, the waiter had remained unnoticed over by the bar. Suddenly, the servant leapt up and ran, aiming to fling himself into space over the edge of the tower. Before the unhinged brute could fall headlong over the crenellation, the sparkling swarm of changelings restrained the pained man in a powerful, fluttering cloud.

"You saw *what?*" The wee Queen calmed the distraught man with a *pooooof* of golden starlight as her minions wafted him back onto *The Citadel* patio floor.

"*Red! R-r-red beeeeast!*" He wept uncontrollably. "*...and G-g-g-genie!*" He could utter no more, and sat rocking in shock and cleaning his teeth obsessively with a flossie.

"Rest now," Queen Elizabeth quieted the nattering swain, then whispered, "Subdue him." With a single, time-tested gesture, the tiny fairy

Queen ordered her most miniscule minions to fly up the nose and out the ears of the distraught waiter. Therein, they slathered his sinuses with a soporific residue.

It was unclear to Queen Elizabeth what had become of Genie. If the dragon did abduct Genie, then the comatose Dragon Slayer was needed right now. Yet, the fairy queen believed that the Genie was essential to reviving Achilles. So, she dispatched a phalanx of fairies to locate the only remaining citizen of the Pink Sand Dead Sea Desert Oasis who had not yet been accounted for that morning, the *Bedouin Medicine Man*. Perhaps he knew Genie's whereabouts. And, leaving Achilles the Dragon Slayer asleep, all set out with a wing and a prayer.

Toward sunset of Slayer's Day 3, the distant smoke tendrils from the flaring nostrils of The Vilest Crimson Dragon subsided; the predator was hungry for Mirage Mountain villagers. For a short time Achilles lay watching the crepuscular start of the beastly fireworks on the horizon: Poor villagers' homes torched with each incandescent display from the marauding dragon swarm.

Genie's MIA: Achilles thought. Cotton-mouthed and alone at *The Citadel Bar*, our groggy Hero revived from his hangover a second time. His gut told him he must rally and venture imminently to the fiend's lair. Unsteadily at first, Our Hero rose from the bench upon which the citizens of The Oasis had laid his magnificent slumbering form. He plotted, *While The Vilest Crimson Dragon pillages the mountain villages, I'll go lay in wait. I'll sequester within its lair until the putrid predator returns to rest. Then, I shall strike. At dawn!*

But without the Genie and Knotty the Magic Carpet, how, *before* dawn, could Slayer cross the desert to reach The Vilest Crimson Dragon's mountain lair? *My steed, I must fetch my rental steed*. And so, wobbly-legged, he jogged to the stables despite his aching Achilles heel.

"Forgive me, Sir, I'm under orders to detain your steed," informed the stable boy.

"Lad," barked Slayer, "saddle my thoroughbred now, or I'll have your job."

The lad feared the outcome were he to disobey Genie's strict orders. "Sir, I cannot release the horse."

"Why?"

"Genie said—"

"Genie? Lad, Genie has been kidnapped!"

Quickly, the wide-eyed ostler saddled up and turned over the reins to the Dragon Slayer. Thereupon, Achilles nuzzled the handsome horse, and removed the copper snaffle bit from its mouth.

"Keep it," he said, handing the wet metal back to the stable boy. "We'll traverse best without restraints."

Our fearless Hero set out across the long shadowed wolds of sun-kissed desert. Despite his hangover, he was looking utterly hot on the back of that stunning fleet-footed Arabian stallion that was by far outmatched in every way by the Dragon Slayer himself. And the horse knew it. Regrettably, not even one impressionable nomadic fan was out strolling the desert to take in Achilles' grandeur. But Slayer did not care. His only thought was to save the Genie.

Galloping across salty pink sands, Our Hero obsessed about how to reach The Vilest Crimson Dragon's rancorous lair before dawn to slay it by surprise. Oh, but the Pink Salt Dead Sea Desert was eternal for a single horse. And night had fallen sharply.

In a fateful moment, the thoroughbred got spooked and bolted headlong into a salty pink dune. Slayer was thrown from the steed. Wiping his mouth, he tasted blood. Above him, the air stirred and frothed, beaten by wings. His gaze shot skyward. He prepared for a dragon attack.

In an iridescent flash, silence fell upon him. And the Queen of the fairies alighted on his shoulder like a songbird. Her minions rested too, tangling themselves in the horse's mane and swinging from its tail.

"Thankfully, you've recovered, Slayer," the diminutive fairy Queen chimed, "in time to help us with a new challenge! I fear that Genie has been taken by the Vilest Crimson Dragon."

"Your Royal Highness, I'm going now on that very rescue mission," replied Slayer. "I shall slay the dragon and save the Genie."

"Are you aware that even this fine steed won't get you there in time?"

"Your Royal Highness, I—"

"I know." She cut him off. "You're trying. But, you're too slow."

"What options have I, Your Majesty?"

"In a heartbeat, Achilles, my strongest changelings and I can transport you to the far mountain range."

"Thank you, Your Royal Hi—"

"I'm not done speaking!" Queen Elizabeth replied irascibly. "Our safe return is gravely imperiled."

"How can I help you, Queen Elizabeth?" Achilles listened closely.

"Such distance we can do one-way, *to* or *fro*, you see... our priceless fairy dust isn't diesel."

"What's your price?" asked Slayer respectfully.

"Fairy dust..." replied the Royal matter-of-factly, "We require sufficient fairy dust to reach and return from the Mirage Mountains."

"Your Majesty, how much is that?"

"Equivalent to a king's ransom." She expected Achilles was shrewd enough to read between her lines.

Wisely, Slayer recognized the Queen's discrete bid that he should pay her emolument with the entire cave filled with priceless treasure of The Vilest Crimson Dragon. Without a doubt, Slayer knew that his friendship with Genie was worth every last dragon's cache on earth. He did not, however, mention *this*, as he elected to leave himself room to negotiate with the fairy Queen if need be. Diplomatically and at once, Achilles conceded to the Queen's request as he removed the saddle from his mighty steed and gave it a soothing *pat-a-pat*.

"Dear Queen Elizabeth of the Beloved Fairies," Slayer began. "I want only a happy life and prosperity for you and your team. Already, you helped me by bringing me into The Oasis where I've experienced bliss and friendship beyond measure. I beg you to help me now to cross the desert." Before the impatient little waif could interrupt him, Slayer completed laying out his terms. "The Vilest Crimson Dragon's treasure is yours, dear Queen. In fact, a tithe of cache of *all* my future slays shall be yours, as well, if Genie lives." He, thereby, left the Queen no wiggle room for doubt or a buyer's remorse bout of sovereign entitlement. Lest she ask for a higher percentage, he nailed down their deal fair and square.

"Agreed," said the hovering sovereign. "Let's be off, then, shall we?

Slayer freed the Arabian back to The Oasis. And then he found himself aloft, buoyed along swifter than any thoroughbred through the bituminous night sky far above all dragons' radar—upon a thunder-head of glittering fairies.

"To the dragon's lair!" The miniscule sparking Queen led the charge toward a dawn of doom, and soothed, "Sleep deeply now, Slayer, or we shall all perish at the pleasure of The Vilest Crimson Dragon."

As Our Hero drifted off to sleep on the fairy cloud, he recalled that it *remained for him to receive his Singular Wish on the Fourth Day*—that is, to get the *One Wish* stored in the Genie's lamp!—*the One Wish Slayer had hoped for all his life, the One Wish he had revealed to no one in the world—ever!* But right now, *that Singular Wish* was the least of his concerns.

Right now, he sought to save his massive friend from the menace of the meanest, canniest, reddest dragon. And to do so, he intended to skewer the cretinous critter after its final night on this earth laying waste to innocent villagers.

But what if Genie's already been consumed? Weeping quietly at the likelihood that his dearest friend was no more, Slayer cried himself to sleep.

Shortly before sunrise, the band of fairies drew near the craggy Mirage Mountains (so called as they were rumored by the simpler Oasis dwellers never to have existed at all for their pinnacle was too high to see). Flying closest to Achilles' face, Queen Elizabeth regarded him as he slept. She smiled to herself recalling that back in the day, Achilles' last name was considered too complicated for preliterate folk. In his native language, it was, formally, *Achilles of the Land Reachable Only by Corsair*.

"And fairies," mused the tiny queen, recalling her visit to Achilles' home, seeking to convince him to come dragon stalking at the Mirage Mountains.

At the time, Slayer had declined in favor of attending his children's sports events. On repeated visits to sway him, Queen Elizabeth had learned that his own people referred to him as *Achilles von Landescorsair*. At last, Slayer had accepted her invitation. When he traveled far from home, the name that stuck was *Dragon Slayer*, and more often than not, simply *Slayer*. On occasion fans rumored that Our Hero Achilles the Dragon Slayer descended from Achilles, the great grandson of Zeus. But,

Queen Elizabeth knew that Slayer was no relation to Greek Achilles for she had known *that* one. That one had taken out Prince Hector in the Trojan War, and readily crushed Poseidon's son Cycnus. In fact, Queen Elizabeth recalled, twenty-four notable foes had fallen at his hand. Even so, she had long ago determined him to be useless at dragon eradication. She decided the two Achilles were similar only insofar as both had the luxury of a personal Bard. And lately Our Hero Achilles did have that pesky issue with his Achilles heel. Yet Slayer Achilles, Queen Elizabeth opined, was braver and smarter by far, gifted in all ways, more fleet-of-foot, light-years more worldly, kind, generous, witty, a fine debater of history, and jaw-dropping by anyone's standard in a Fibonacci Golden Ratio way. Wherever Slayer went, he easily passed *go* and happily collected ransom after king's ransom.

As the black sky faded to pale orange-pinks and hues of blue, Queen Elizabeth signaled her team to lose altitude. Gently they fluttered and coasted until they touched down. On a stone outcropping near the entrance to The Vilest Crimson Dragon's cave, they lay Achilles. Thereupon, he awoke choking on exhaust from his means of transport—a pother of fairy dust!

"Enough with the glitter, I'm ready!" Slayer forced a smile and strode straight to the lair of The Vilest Crimson Dragon. *My smile is my shield*, he recalled the words of his own fine mother far away in the land reachable only by Corsair.

"Good luck, Achilles! We love you!" sang the swooning band of tiny winged fairies before they fled into hiding behind a nearby waterfall. There they rested and rehydrated their wings for the return journey—all praying that Slayer and Genie survived. If not, Queen Elizabeth would need to find a way to manufacture more fairy dust without being torched by dragons.

"I'm ready!" Achilles declared again, this time with greater confidence as he made tracks inside the gaping cave. Stalactites and stalagmites seemed to gnash at him like mammoth jaws. He did not care. *Right now*, he thought, *I'm saving Genie*.

"I'm sooooo ready!" Dragon Slayer Achilles sped down the tunnel to the bowels of the dragon's lair. The deeper the darker and soon he could barely see. Sunrise meant the return of the dragon. Achilles had to act fast. He groped in the darkness for a door.

"Here, Achilles, take this." Queen Elizabeth swooped in swift as a swift and palmed him a flaming *torchier*. He thanked her as she sped away and out to the waterfall to join her minions.

Readily, Slayer broke the iron hasp locking a door that led to the inner sanctum of The Vilest Crimson Dragon's home. Underfoot there clinked gold galleons strewn haphazardly on the stone floor. Piles of glittering ore were punctuated by the skeletal remains of fallen attackers of the wily winged worm.

"*Do I stay or do I—?*" Lyrics clashed in the mind of Slayer Achilles as he glanced back at the long tunnel behind him. Mere minutes remained until dawn and inevitable combat with the vilest, reddest beast.

Singular focus pulled him deeper. Advancing into the dragon's nest, Slayer's piercing chestnut eyes gleamed brighter than the treasures he ignored. He tripped over middens of gold bars, each embossed with the crest of a different fallen ruler. Some even bore inscriptions in Cuneiform. And rather many, as well, hailed from the ancient tribe of diminutive Amazon fairies who had once ruled the earth with their kindness before big people got avaricious and took over. The Oasis was the waifs' last stronghold. Slayer looked forward to gifting all the treasure to the hummingbird-size fairy Queen and her team who had buoyed him across the desert.

Advancing deeper down inside the fetid cave, along a far wall obscured by a gold monolith, Slayer noticed what appeared to be The Vilest Crimson Dragon's primary feeding area. Apart from scattered bones and scraps of fetid offal, there, Achilles noticed three large iron doors. He wondered what lay behind each and to what destination the doors might lead. *Perhaps a passage through the mountain to the fairies' waterfall? Or an underground escape hatch back to The Oasis?*

Chains rattled in a dangerous corner beyond a heap of gemstones, loot'n booty that glistened in concert with Achilles' *torchier. Perhaps it's Genie*, Achilles heart leapt with hope and he climbed over the treasure spoils to discover a lovely line of maidens in flowy satin dresses chained and asleep.

Dragon's breakfast, thought Achilles ruefully, *I must free them.*

Meanwhile, also in heavy chains, slumped in a heap, Genie was despondent—locked behind one of the three large iron doors—only a few desperate meters from the Dragon Slayer.

Useless, the magic lamp lay out of reach, tied to the Magic Carpet that had been bound—and gagged!—by The Vilest Crimson Dragon. The reason being that carpets, back in those days, had a reputation for mouthing off insouciantly and escaping—unlike the apathetic lay-about carpets of today, that serve only to cover floors.

Dawn was nigh and Day Four was upon them. Therefore, Slayer Achilles' Wish Fulfillment was ripe. And Genie, dear benevolent Genie, was really so very sad to be indisposed, and thus, unable to deliver Achilles' *one* earthly wish. *What...?* Genie wondered. *What does a guy who already has it all even wish for?* Genie was stymied and really, really wanted to know what Slayer's One Wish would turn out to be. Decisively, Genie planned, *If I escape this dragon drama, I know just what I'll do with Slayer. The moment I'm free of the dragon's magic spell, I shall first plant the biggest kiss on Achilles and later explain my icky personal complications... To beg forgiveness*, Genie reasoned, *is more prudent than to ask permission.* The thought drew a pale smile to the Genie's full lips.

But first, Genie had to save... well, Genie. This Genie had pulled a hat-rabbit one time too many for it to hold the slightest intrigue or life lesson. *Been there done that.* Given that The Oasis was replete with eunuchs whose prospect of *growing a set* was nil, Genie had been waiting an inordinately long time for a real hero to step up to the plate—*Defend my honor, already!* Indelibly instilled with a hybrid Grimm-Disney princess rescue complex, Genie believed Slayer's help alone would break the red dragon's imprisonment spell. It was a spell that had ensnared Genie's entire being for such a long time that no one, including Queen Elizabeth, even remembered who Genie had been *before* the spell was cast. And what made The Vilest Crimson Dragon's spell more effective was that it gas-lighted Genie from asking anyone for help, including the magic lamp.

Dragons were predictable and Genie had known to keep away from them. But somehow Genie had got snookered when The Vilest Crimson Dragon had slithered up all *lambie-wolf-in-sheepskin* having shape-shifted into a kindly, self-effacing gentleman—for apparent courtship purposes, as dragons are wont to do (so beware!). It was not until *after* the dragon had swept Genie away that the crimson captor proved to be an hirsute booze-hound, and a mean-spirited apex predator. The very beast whom all potential quarry of Genie's genteel *milieu* had been taught by watchful parents never to trust: The dishonorable dragon had won.

Time and again, Genie had tried to escape the vile reptile's cruel propensity to gas-light, and so, ultimately, in an effort to control Genie's every move, the red lizard transmogrified the otherwise-unencumbered young professional into a shape-shackled Genie condemned to an eternity of granting brass lamp wishes to strangers. While Genie did, in fact, enjoy the happy outcome of granting wishes, better things remained to do than rot away in a dragon's lair under its dreadful spell inside the Mirage Mountains at the farthest edge of the Pink Salt Dead Sea Desert. Genie spat violently at the merest shadow of a thought of the repellent reptile's return.

At that moment, in the dim light, Genie noticed hefty bolt cutters buried partially in a heap of gold rubble. Sadly, the abridged span of chains binding Genie's hands and bare feet left the bolt cutters slightly out of reach. Once the tool *du jour* of a long-ago-digested bicycle thief, the shears now became Genie's only hope of escape.

"Knotty, see if you can budge!" ordered Genie. "A little closer and I can try to—" But Knotty the Magic Carpet was asleep. "Carpet! Wake *up*!" yelled Genie, sharp and loud.

"*Genie?!*" queried a hopeful voice outside the cell door, a voice that stirred not only Knotty the Magic Carpet from its slumber, but the very core of Genie's soul.

"*Slayer?!*" Breathless, Genie strained for the bolt cutters. "Get me out!"

Relieved, Dragon Slayer Achilles ran his hands over Genie's iron door seeking to pry it open. "I'm here to save you, Genie!" His every word was manna-balm to Genie's sad heart.

Slayer's crescendo of relief that welled inside him was immediately short-circuited by some serious s*** and I do mean serious s*** that erupted right then! The fair maidens in chains screamed in terror. *That*, in and of itself, was worse than nails on a chalkboard. And poor Slayer Achilles was acutely sensitive to high-pitched sound. Their *arpeggio* of royal keening ensued *da capo*, and provided a backdrop to a *canon* of enervating wailing by one princess, punctuated by ear-splitting *szforzando* shrieks by another. And so trilled the cacophonous symphony that unleashed itself in the very moment Achilles felt the first blast of dragon fire. Laser heat drilled home the news that the sun had crept o're the horizon. And with it, The Vilest Crimson Dragon. Red and mad, its predilection for death was categorically *not* at the hand of the nemesis of all dragons.

Instinctively, Achilles dove behind a large pile of gold bars for protection while he corralled his thoughts. *At least Genie's safe behind that iron door*, he thought, *even if the maidens and I myself should immolate presently*. The pile of gold bars shielding Slayer liquefied in a puddle of golden goo with the second seething-hot projectile from his fiery foe. Achilles' hope refueled by Genie's voice, Slayer feared nought. Now, more confident than ever, he was very eager to get the job done and get back to having fun with his infatuate ensconced behind door number three.

Dragon Slayer

10

Genie studied the change in light and heat emanating through the gap between the threshold and the bottom of the cell door when all of a sudden a revelation befell the captive thaumaturge.

"Mind the gap, Knotty!" Genie exclaimed.

"Genie, you're delirious," remarked the snarky Magic Carpet.

Hands chained, Genie pointed adamantly at the gap at the base of the heavy door. Its threshold increased in breadth on account of molten gold that seared away every rock lump and dust speck in its path. From Genie's vantage point, the dragon's sudden fire bursts were a blessing, summoning a chance of escape as the gap grew larger.

"The gap, Knotty, the gap! Escape through it! Scroll up tight," instructed Genie. "Your ropes might slip away!"

With that, the Magic Carpet curled itself into a scroll, compressing its plush nap. And its bonds *did* fall away. Behind it remained the magic brass lamp in a tangle of rope and gold bits. The finely-knotted masterpiece unfurled across the floor—a generous 9' x 12' exquisite for high altitude picnics. Then it hurled itself lavishly about the rafters, picking up speed, and bloviating, "I am *Naughty-Naughty Knotty!*"

"Distract the dragon!" ordered Genie, "Go!"

Valiantly, lithe Knotty aimed to slide under the door. *Swoosh!* In a jerk, just at the threshold, the Magic Carpet balked.

"I'm scared, Genie, I'll singe my fringe," choked the Magic Carpet curling up beside Genie whose otherwise compassionate baby blues flew into an eye-roll.

"*Lay-about*," muttered Genie.

Perhaps two minutes remained for grace to step in and free those trapped inside the lair of the cruelest creature on earth. The bristling red buzzard was still beastly hungry after an exhilarating night scorching terrorized troglodytes. Nimbly, valorous Achilles sprang beyond the dragon's next meal—that being the screaming satin-clad maidens in chains. Knightly Slayer intended to return the ear-splitting youths to the benevolent king who ruled way over by the seaside at the far end of the pink salt desert, three-weeks' ride on a thoroughbred from The Oasis. Honor bound, Slayer vowed to do it. The thought of three weeks on a horse, in a desert, accompanied by orchestrated quailing and shrillness: That was not for him, no, not a't'all. Yet he knew that saving divas destined for dragon dinner was the right thing to do. And the king's reward for his princesses' safe return would be grand. Though the reality of such a task invoked pleurisy jaundice in Achilles, he determined to risk it.

As Slayer withdrew into the shadows of the cave, again he pressed his ear to the third door. Indistinct clattering of gold coins obscured the words that pierced his upper left ventricle and amygdala simultaneously, "Slayer, get me out!" *Oh, that dulcet voice.* Slayer had come to treasure the very sound of his friend Genie.

Slayer cleared his head: *slay dragon, rescue Genie*, then get the heck back to the business of having fun with his Brobdingnagian buddy.

"I'll save you, Genie!" A tsunami of gladness and succor scintillated opiates through Slayer's sinewy muscles all the way to his toes, and strong fingertips that gripped his mortiferous sword.

Intending to pry off its hinges, our valiant Hero leveraged his blade upon the cell door. At that very moment, not only did the chained nobles scream louder (that in and of itself was akin to aural waterboarding), BUT... an ear-searing *hisssssssss*, louder and faster than the speed of light, obliterated the royal keening.

In a heartbeat, another fireball took out Doors 1 and 2, right beside Dragon Slayer. Achilles turned to face the monster.

"*Ha!* Missed me, *Scarlet!*" taunted Achilles, and dove behind a wall of gold bars, thus dodging stridulant incineration.

"It's *Crimson* to you!" snorted the haughty dragon. Home in a disastrous mood, it was ravenous; the mountain folk had become savvier at hiding from the vehement behemoth.

In that brief shielded moment behind a king's ransom of gold bars, Our Hero strategized ever faster. Then it occurred to him:

Alas, with the previous blast from the dragon's infernal maw, the royal maidens were toast. At least the cave was quiet, apart from the gold that sizzled across the floor. *And Genie's safe*, Slayer reassured himself. Eager to get the job done and go play with Genie, Achilles surveyed options for their exeunt: The main tunnel plus three doors—*surely one of these must egress to a secret passage.*

Another fireball liquefied the massive gold monolith behind which Achilles hunkered. A pool of glitter seeped further across the stone floor, smoking-hot, searing all in its wake. Though our brave Slayer feared not, he was now fully and irretrievably exposed with nothing to protect him but his sword and his swagger, his very clever wits, breath-taking brawn, and rakish grin.

"Can't you do better than that, *Ruby?*" Slayer's brilliant smile lit up his patrician features as he sauntered directly toward the red malediction. Goading the hoary abomination with feigned indifference, Our Hero Achilles slung his sword casually palming it hand-to-hand.

"Bring it, Beast!"

Meanwhile on the other side of Door 3, Genie had managed to loosen the bolt cutters from under a pile of gold galleons bearing the profiles of queens, kings, and heads of banking families who had long since opted to reside under a pseudonym for their own collective safety. Alas, cutting the chain proved a problem, for Genie's hands remained bound and Knotty, of course, hadn't any. Yet the carpet and all its tassels gave a fluttery shove to the cutters. That brought them close enough for Genie to snag with prehensile toes.

"You've got to help Slayer, Carpet, go! Now! Through the gap!"

Reluctantly, Knotty scrolled up again, more compact than before. Sure enough, the tighter Carpet spiraled, the swifter spun its arabesques in the confined space. In a sparkling dust cloud, Knotty Carpet shook itself out and whipped about the chamber, gaining speed as it angled at its widening escape hatch beneath the door.

"Go, Knotty!" yelled Genie urgently as the door smoldered with a wave of smelted gold and iron seeping across its threshold.

In one quick fringe-singe-ing *glissade*, the Magic Carpet escaped out the gap. The kamikaze rug divebombed the Dragon's head. Knotty eluded snapping jaws, and flew about its bulging eyes. The died-in-the-wool loyal Persian confused the beast just long enough for The Dragon Slayer to deliver an acutely terminal blow between cardinal coriaceous gills. His blade plumbed the dragon's curmudgeonly heart.

The deed was done.

"Thanks, Carpet," cried Achilles joyfully. "Great teamwork. Let's get Genie! Knotty? Knotty? Knotty! *Oh, no!*" A posthumous fireball had vaporized Knotty whose intrepid spirit continued to chase and fluster that of the infernal avian worm, far into the hereafter.

The Vilest Crimson Dragon's last exhalation had liquefied the door to Genie's cell, and melted the gold upon which Genie sat. "*Ouchie!*" yelled Genie leaping up. The boiling liquid floor seared away the chains. Genie scurried against the back wall where the stone floor remained just warm enough to stand.

And in the instant that the dragon choked out its final fetid fumes, death terminated The Vilest Crimson Dragon's imprisonment spell on Genie. Vanquished, the beleaguering spell went up in a puff of stinky tallow smoke. With it, alas, vaporized Genie's magic dominion over the lamp. The lamp was now without a master. And with the neutralization of Genie's magic, the power to grant Slayer's One Wish remained trapped inside the brass lamp. And that lamp lay helpless on the floor holding its spout shut under a pool of steaming gold.

Awash in a confusing mix of emotions, Genie was exhilarated and saddened. Exhilarated to be free of the heavy burden of Crimson's curse; saddened to be unable to grant Slayer's One Wish. Oh how Genie had looked forward to doing so. Still, Genie was dying to know what on earth Achilles could possibly want.

"I'm free, Slayer, you freed me!" hollered Genie, approaching carefully from the back of the third cell.

Hearing Genie's voice, Slayer's chest heaved in relief. He turned from the shuddering dragon corpse.

"Genie?" Achilles exclaimed dumbfounded. "*You're* not…"

"Yes, I *am*, Slayer."

"You're *not*… Where's Genie?"

"Slayer, I *am* Genie!"

Slayer gazed into the sparkling blue eyes brimming with Genie's spirited mirth—that much he recognized! But Genie's phenotype had pulled a 180, from endomorph to ectomorph, and…

"But you're— not a, a—dude. And you're not, wait— How's this possib—?" He caught his breath as he took in Genie's transformed silhouette, diminutive compared to Genie's larger-than-life being that Slayer had come to expect and adore.

"I'll explain," Genie assured Slayer, jonesing to plant that fantasy smooch on him. "Help me get past the flames."

Together Slayer and Genie broke into a giggle fit as they beheld one another spellbound through the flames that separated them by just a few feet. They could not reach one another fast enough. But it seemed to be taking forever.

Have you ever had one of those labyrinthine dreams wherein endless effort is required to get back to the place or person you so dearly wanted to reach in the first place? Wherein each turn mushrooms into a *Hydra of Hazards*, speedbumps down frightful Alice in Wonderland rabbit tunnels, wherein every new variable takes you farther and farther and then ever farther away from the place or person you want most to reach? And yet you slog onward—just to reach your *objet de désir*!

So too did Achilles persist as he reached for Genie. *Flames be damned!* Slayer thrust his hand through the incendiary toward her.

"Give me your hand, Genie, I'll pull you through to this side of the flames."

Hopeful, they both laughed happily because they'd won! Together they had beaten the vile foe who had interrupted their fun at *The Citadel Bar & Grill*. And again, they believed, they could now, at last, go play together.

But... in a whiplash moment, they both paused to regard each other. At first in wonder. And then, with fear. In any event, in the latter portion of that same slow-mo-moment, Genie disappeared altogether.

"*Nooooooo!*" yelled Slayer.

"*Slayerrrrrrrrrrrrrrrrrrrrrrrrrrrrr,*" screamed Genie.

What had happened?

A nano-Planck—or perhaps it was a few Planck units of time. Had Slayer reached for Genie one shaved Planck unit faster, instead of gazing at her pulchritude for ten Planck units, he might have saved her. But he dallied. Okay, he didn't exactly *dally*; Slayer was no slacker. Yet, there lapsed a pulsing lag. Call it bad timing... one sigh too long as he stared at his friend, taking in every centimeter of her comely visage, restored to its original resplendence. He thrilled at Genie's beauty. But his excitement foundered, then anatomized in a vexing quiescence of disappointment. *Disappointment?* Slayer couldn't understand. *Why?!* This new original Genie was healthy, fit, radiantly pretty, not to mention, eager to kiss him. Even so, Slayer wanted his buddy back, his *compadre* with whom he felt free and able to laugh at his fears. Now, *now*, this luscious maiden stood before him—Slayer feared in that split-Planck moment—*she'll have expectations of me. She'll want me to fulfill her knight rescue fantasies, toe the line, bite the bit. Won't she? Don't they all?* Vague constrictive images of bridle, reins, saddle, whip, and spurs overtook him from a past life as a sleek ebony Friesian thoroughbred show horse—one that longed to *spit the bit*.

In that Planck unit of time while Slayer struggled with genderist confusion, Genie was having her own bout of disappointment. Of course, Genie was thrilled to have been saved from olde Crimson's curse. She had her own body back, which felt great, and she ached to share it with Slayer. She adored everything about him—his laughter, his spontaneity, his kindness and brains, and certainly all that's exquisitely objectifiable about an athletic physique. But when Genie shape-shifted, she saw *that look* in his eyes shift. As dudes, Genie and Slayer had been free bros and homies, carousing every establishment of The Oasis. Slayer had responded freely to Genie's *joie de vivre* and ingenuity. But now, she felt his eyes stop short with raw hunger at her blushing curves and soft surfaces. The freedom she had felt with

Slayer until now simply vaporized. And Genie, again, felt trapped, this time by something far more insidious than a pernicious red dragon's curse: Gender tradition.

Why's it so flipping complicated? Together in that same cataclysmic moment, both Genie and Slayer wondered in lonely silence. It was in that revelatory instant, when Slayer's fingertips touched Genie's, that the solder-hot gold cooked the cell floor out from beneath Genie. And away she fell before Slayer could hyper-extend far enough to draw her steadfastly into his arms to safety, and hold her forever.

"*Noooooo!*" yelled Slayer. "*Geniiiiiie!!!*" was the last she heard of his voice.

Along with gold and melted bolt cutters, Genie was followed by the gold-sodden brass lamp. All dropped away into a heretofore unknown, bottomless hatch, built millennia past by sturdy pink-salt-mining dwarves believed to be extinct dragon-fodder, until this very day.

"*Slayerrrrrrrrrrrrrrrrrrrrrrrr!*" screamed Genie as she plummeted.

Staring down from the rim of the abyss, Slayer was bereft...

G.G. Garth

— until —

Dragon Slayer

...the next installment of *The Official & Historically-Accurate Saga of Achilles the Dragon Slayer of the Pink Salt Dead Sea Desert.*

Coming Soon

Dragon Slayer

About the Author

G.G. Garth is Ghia Truesdale's *nom de plume* for her adult fairy tales, DRAGON SLAYER OF THE PINK SAND DEAD SEA DESERT and HAT RABBIT WISH, and tetralogy of vintage thrillers for young adults, NIGHTMARE MATINEE, DRIVEN TO KILL!, BAD DOG: A VAMPIRE'S CANINE, and PARTY TILL YOU SCREAM!. Ghostwriter and development-editor of over 50 books for other best-selling and respected authors, including Sean Patrick Flanery's JANE TWO, Armin Shimerman's ILLYRIA: BETRAYAL OF ANGELS, Ben Levin's IN THE HOLE and NELLIE'S FRIENDS, Mr. Brainwash, Hunt Slonem, Robert Mars, Ted Vassilev, Halim Flowers, Stephen Wilson, John L'Heureux, Theodore Weesner, Mel King, Latif Bossman, Konrad Bercovici, Kit Brennan, Victoria Griffith, Susan Levin, Charles Brady, and R. Scott Bernard. She has two phenomenal children, her best creations, and lives in New England.

AWESOME! Very interesting, many twists and turns that made me want to keep reading—imaginative, impressive, terrific!
—Ben Levin, Author, *IN THE HOLE*

I became immersed in the enviable narrative... Impressively extensive skill weaving a colorful and engrossing tale, mixing traditional and modern themes in a compelling, contemporaneous tale for adults. Effortlessly, G.G. Garth paints vivid characters and unforgettable landscapes. Keeps reader on edge, asking, "What next?" Leaves reader hungry for more... combines a dream quality with sharp realism that takes the reader to a time of innocence, dragons, and uncertainty, yet hopeful...
—Ramesh Gupta a/k/a Haemish McGee, Author
The Mountain of Gold and
Ballad of a Poor Man's Reward.

Made in the USA
Middletown, DE
31 May 2022